First printing, February 2022

Illustrations copyright © 2022 by Eleanor Jones.

ISBN 979-8-9856114-0-3 (paperback)
ISBN 979-8-9856114-1-0 (hardcover)

www.danishahuntley.com

LOST LAND

by
Danisha Huntley

Illustrated by Eleanor Jones

Amora turned her room upside down
in an effort to find her favorite doll, Holly Elizabeth.
She was afraid that Holly was now in Lost Land.
After a toy goes missing, they're transported to Lost Land
to live out the rest of their days.

She'd only heard stories about Lost Land,
but she'd never had one of her own toys live there!
"Holly Elizabeth really needs me!" cried Amora.
"She's not used to being by herself."

Amora decided to take a brave journey to Lost Land
in hopes of finding her favorite doll.
As she walked down the sidewalk,
her surroundings started to change.
The pavement turned bright orange!
The clouds dazzled with sparkles in them
and trees grew gorgeous flowers.

As she walked further down,
she ran into tall gates blocking her from entering the land.
"I'm locked out!" said Amora.
"I need to find a way to get through these gates!"

And then, out of nowhere, a little boy appeared with a shiny crown on his head. It was Jacob Jerome. King of Lost Land. Only the king had the powers to open the gates.
"Hello there!" said the king.
"We don't get visitors often here in Lost Land. How can I help you?"

"My favorite doll, Holly Elizabeth, is trapped in Lost Land!"
said Amora. "Can you please let me inside?"
The king was happy to help.
He turned and pointed at the gates.
Magic shot out from his finger and the gates began to open.

Amora walked through the gates and stared in amazement
at how stunning Lost Land was.
"Lost Land is enormous! How am I ever going to find Holly?"
Amora worried.

"We'll find her," said the king. "We just have to keep a positive attitude and we won't give up! What's an activity that Holly Elizabeth loved to do?"
"Hmm?" Amora thought,
"Oh I know! She loved to play dress up!"
"She could be playing dress up at the local boutique here in Lost Land!"
said the king.
"Let's go and find out!"

With the snap of his fingers, King Jacob Jerome transported Amora and himself to Razzle Dazzle, the local boutique of Lost Land. They both walked around the store calling out Holly's name. "Holly? Holly? Are you here?"

The store clerk overheard them.
"Are you two looking for Holly Elizabeth?"
asked the clerk. "Yes we are!" Amora said.
"Is she here?" "She was here earlier today."
said the clerk. "I helped her pick out the perfect outfit!
She got hungry so she went off to find lunch."

King Jacob asked Amora
what was Holly's favorite food
to eat. "She loves pizza!"
said Amora. "She must be at
the local pizza place!" said the king.
He snapped his fingers and they
both landed at Poppin' Pizza,
the best pizza place in Lost Land.

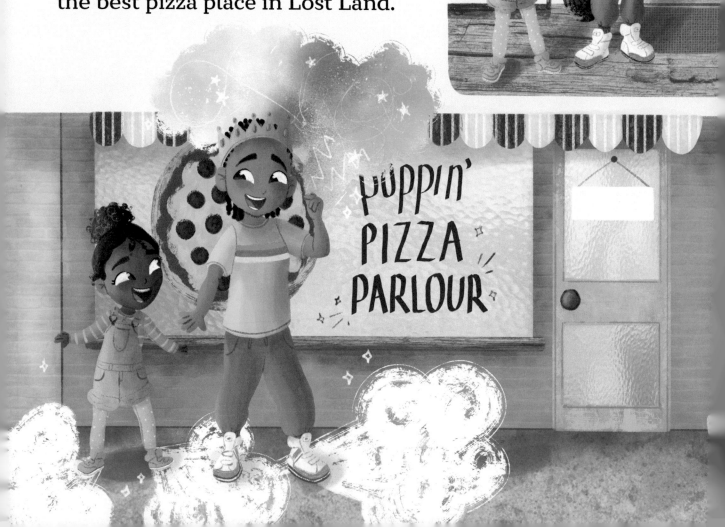

POPPIN'
PIZZA
PARLOUR

When they got there, they both saw that Holly was nowhere in the restaurant. They asked the pizza man if he had seen a doll named Holly Elizabeth.

"Oh yes!" said the pizza man.

"She ordered a pepperoni pizza to-go. She said that she plans on having a picnic at the park!"

Amora and King Jacob ran off to the park as they yelled,
"Thank you!" to the pizza man.
At the park, they spotted picnic tables and ran to them.
They asked the teddy bears sitting there
if they'd seen a doll named Holly.

"She was here eating pizza!" said one of the bears.
"When she left, she said she was off to find some books to read.
You two should check the library."
Amora and King Jacob thanked the bears for the tip
and hurried off to the library of Lost Land.

They called out Holly's name in every section of the library, but still no sign of her. Amora asked the librarian if she had seen a doll named Holly Elizabeth. "She was here a moment ago." explained the librarian. "She left with her hands full of books."

"Did she say where she was going?" asked the king.
"She said she was going home to do some reading."
said the librarian. "Home?" questioned Amora.
"Holly has her own home here in Lost Land?"
"Yes, she does." said the king.
"Every toy in Lost Land has a home of its own.
We have an entire neighborhood of doll houses.
Let's go there and try to find Holly's house!"

King Jacob Jerome used his magic to take them both to Elegant Hills. This neighborhood was filled with beautiful homes for every doll in Lost Land. "We must ring every door bell, and hopefully, Holly will answer one of these doors." said the king. So together, they rang **99** doorbells! And still, no Holly.

At the 100th house, a beautiful doll with bright eyes and a big smile opened the door. It was Holly Elizabeth! "Holly! We found you!" said Amora. "Amora!" said Holly. "How did you find me? I didn't know humans could live in Lost Land, too!"

"King Jacob and I searched all over Lost Land to find you!" said Amora. I'm here to take you home with me where you belong."

All of a sudden, Holly's bright smile faded and she became sad.

"What's wrong Holly? You've been in Lost Land all by yourself. Aren't you happy to come home with me?"

"I've missed you a great deal." said Holly.
"But I'm home here in Lost Land. I'm the happiest I've ever been!
I get to do all of the things I love to do. And I've made great
friends along the way!"

Amora was disappointed to hear this news from her favorite doll,
but she loved Holly so much that her happiness mattered most.
She decided to let Holly Elizabeth stay in Lost Land.
Amora asked the king if she could ever come and visit Holly again.

The king snapped his fingers and a shiny crown appeared on the top of Amora's head. "You have shown great selflessness and compassion." said King Jacob. "Those are great qualities to have as the princess of Lost Land!" "Am I really a princess?" Amora asked.

"Yes!" the king proclaimed. "You are now Princess of Lost Land. You have the power to open the gates and enter Lost Land at any time!" With a big smile, Amora thanked King Jacob Jerome and gave Holly Elizabeth a warm hug. But they did not say goodbye, because they would surely see each other again.

Made in the USA
Columbia, SC
03 February 2024

31328540R00018